W9-ACX-218

James Bear and the Goose Gathering

For The Hungry Mind
—J.L.

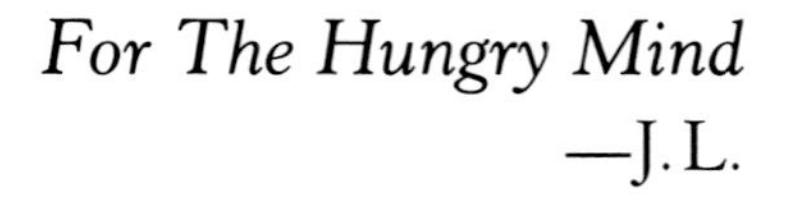

For my own James Bear,
my husband, Jim
—B.F.-F.

Charles Scribner's Sons Books for Young Readers
Macmillan Publishing Company • 866 Third Avenue, New York, NY 10022

Maxwell Macmillan Canada, Inc.
1200 Eglinton Avenue East, Suite 200, Don Mills, Ontario M3C 3N1

Macmillan Publishing Company is part of the
Maxwell Communication Group of Companies.

First edition 10 9 8 7 6 5 4 3 2 1
Printed in Hong Kong

Library of Congress Cataloging-in-Publication Data
Latimer, Jim, date
James Bear and the goose gathering / Jim Latimer ;
pictures by Betsy Franco-Feeney. — 1st ed.
p. cm. — (Charles Scribner's Sons books for young readers)
Summary: Vegetarian Bear, who likes to surprise and entertain both himself and others, this time digs a hole where geese are to gather for fellowship and good feeling—and to hum.
ISBN 0-684-19526-7
[1. Bears—Fiction. 2. Geese—Fiction. 3. Animals—Fiction.]
I. Franco-Feeney, Betsy, ill. II. Title. III. Series.
PZ7.L369617Jak 1994 [E]—dc20 92-26190

James Bear and the Goose Gathering

JIM LATIMER
Pictures by Betsy Franco-Feeney

CHARLES SCRIBNER'S SONS • NEW YORK
Maxwell Macmillan Canada • Toronto
Maxwell Macmillan International
New York • Oxford • Singapore • Sydney

James Bear was a great, pale-furred bear with fire-hydrant feet and paws the size of dinner plates. He was mostly known among his friends as Bear. He was a rugby player, a singer, and a vegetarian, but mostly a vegetarian.

Every day, Bear grazed through acres of herbs and grasses, and sometimes, to entertain himself and give his teeth a rest, he played gentle rugby with the caterpillars and crickets that crawled and hopped in the tall grass. And Bear was a singer in the Trout and Cricket Choir. It was called a trout and cricket choir though there were caterpillars in it, too. And there was Bear—and Buffalo.

"But," Bear's friend Skunk wanted to know, "do you really sing? Do *trout* really sing?"

"Yes and no," Bear answered. There were sixteen river trout in the Trout and Cricket Choir, along with four caterpillars, one hundred crickets, and Bear and Buffalo. On the mornings when it didn't rain, the caterpillars and crickets boarded the shuttle bus (which was really Bear). And then the crickets and the caterpillars and Bear collected the choir trout in buckets—

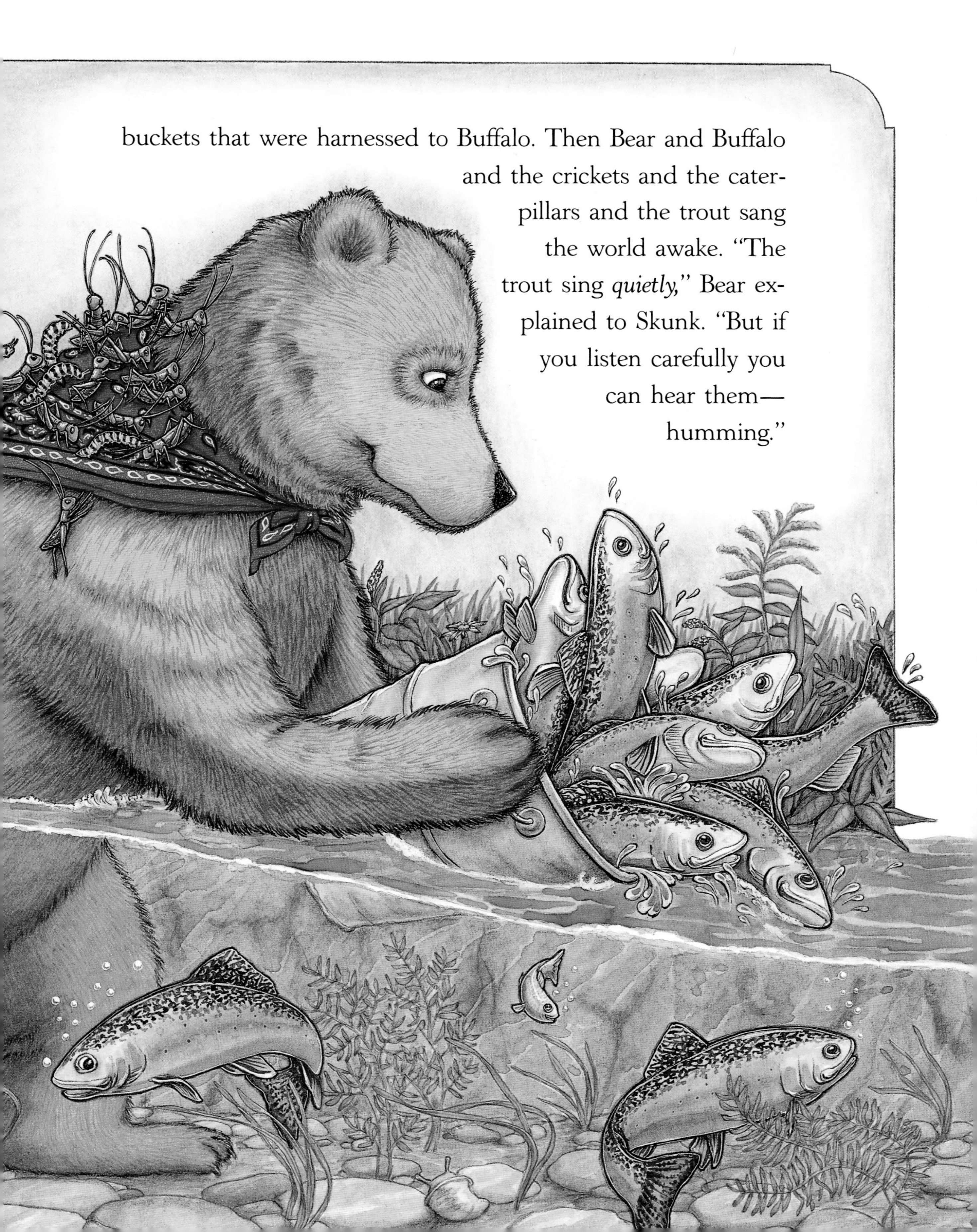

buckets that were harnessed to Buffalo. Then Bear and Buffalo and the crickets and the caterpillars and the trout sang the world awake. "The trout sing *quietly,*" Bear explained to Skunk. "But if you listen carefully you can hear them—humming."

"But do you really play rugby?" Skunk asked. "With caterpillars?"

"Well, yes and no," Bear answered. Bear wore his rugby pants and his rugby jersey. He coached and kept score and clapped his paws. But he played cricket-and-caterpillar-rugby mostly in his mind. And always, when the match was over, or when the world had been sung awake, Bear got down to grazing.

It takes a lot of grazing—a lot of boring herbs and grasses—to support a bear, especially when the bear is getting fat for fall, and sometimes James Bear did other things to surprise and entertain himself. Sometimes he did things to surprise and entertain his neighbors, who were geese.

One pale September morning, Bear lumbered out of the tall grass toward the riverbank. The geese, when he found them, were preening and parading in the watery sunshine. Bear stood watching the geese splash into the water and out again, apparently taking no notice of him. After a moment Bear chose a place on the bank, close to the geese but not too close, and he began to dig.

The pale, cider-colored bear dug a shallow hole, pushing loamy soil out between his legs, sometimes lifting it high above his head. Bear pawed and shoveled, spraying soil in all directions, until a spark of curiosity flared among the geese, until the geese jostled and flapped together to the rim of Bear's hole.

"What?" the geese asked, peering down at him. "What is this?"

"It's a Bear's hole," one goose shouted.

"*Is* it a Bear's hole?" shouted another.

Bear looked at the geese. "Yes and no," he answered.

Yes and no? The geese blinked at him.

"I promised not to tell you," Bear explained.

The geese, astonished, asked Bear whom he had promised.

"Skunk," Bear answered. Bear had promised his friend Skunk that he would stop making up stories to trick the geese. The year before he had told them that a big cottonwood tree growing near the river was a *frowning tree.* Bear and the geese had spent the better part of the year frowning together at the "frowning tree."

But the geese wanted to hear this story.

Bear came out of the hole, but he looked doubtful. He looked nervous.

"Come on," the geese whispered.

"Please," they shouted.

Bear took a breath. "Okay," he told them. "I will tell you."

"Long ago," Bear began, "there was a dream time, a *golden age* for geese." (The geese moved closer together.) "It was a time," Bear said, "when geese were proud and strong, a time of matchless grace and soaring pride; a time when your ancestor geese gathered in great congregations and choirs; a time when goose voices boomed and swelled in song across the land."

"Do you mean we *sang*?" the geese asked.

Bear nodded. "There were tenors and sopranos," he said, "and altos and baritones."

The geese exchanged looks. They honked experimentally, trying for a harmony.

"During the golden age," Bear continued, "geese sang with style, and they walked with grace and rhythm. They walked," Bear said, "in fancy stockings and ballet slippers."

The geese stared at their fly-swatter feet.

"And the goose golden age," Bear said, "was a time when, without molting or preening, geese were *fledged* to perfection. Their feathers were perfect, matchless—in flight, dazzlingly beautiful."

The geese's breasts seemed to swell.

"The golden age," said Bear, "was a time when bread crumbs and popcorn lay everywhere about, a time when geese ate only as they chose and only what they wished. But above all else," Bear said, "the golden age was a time when there were, placed so as to suit a goose's best convenience, *goose gathering places.*"

The geese stared.

"These were holes where geese gathered for fellowship and good feeling," Bear explained. "But bears liked them, too, and when geese gave up gathering in holes, the goose gathering places were taken over by bears—which is the other reason I'm not supposed to tell you."

The geese stood in silence awhile at the edge of Bear's hole. At last one said, "But what did geese do in the holes?"

Bear cocked his head. "Well," he said, "they hummed, for one thing." Bear told the geese their ancestors had had sweet humming voices.

Sweet humming voices. The geese seemed to let this sink in a moment, then they hustled and flapped Bear away from his hole, and jostled and hustled and clambered their way in.

For a moment Bear watched as the geese sorted and arranged themselves. Then he turned toward the tall grass and lumbered off, stopping for a last look by the edge of the riverbank. Bear's last glimpse was of the geese gathered in their hole, bills pointed skyward, humming. But *could* they be humming? Bear wasn't sure. He thought he could hear them when he listened very carefully.

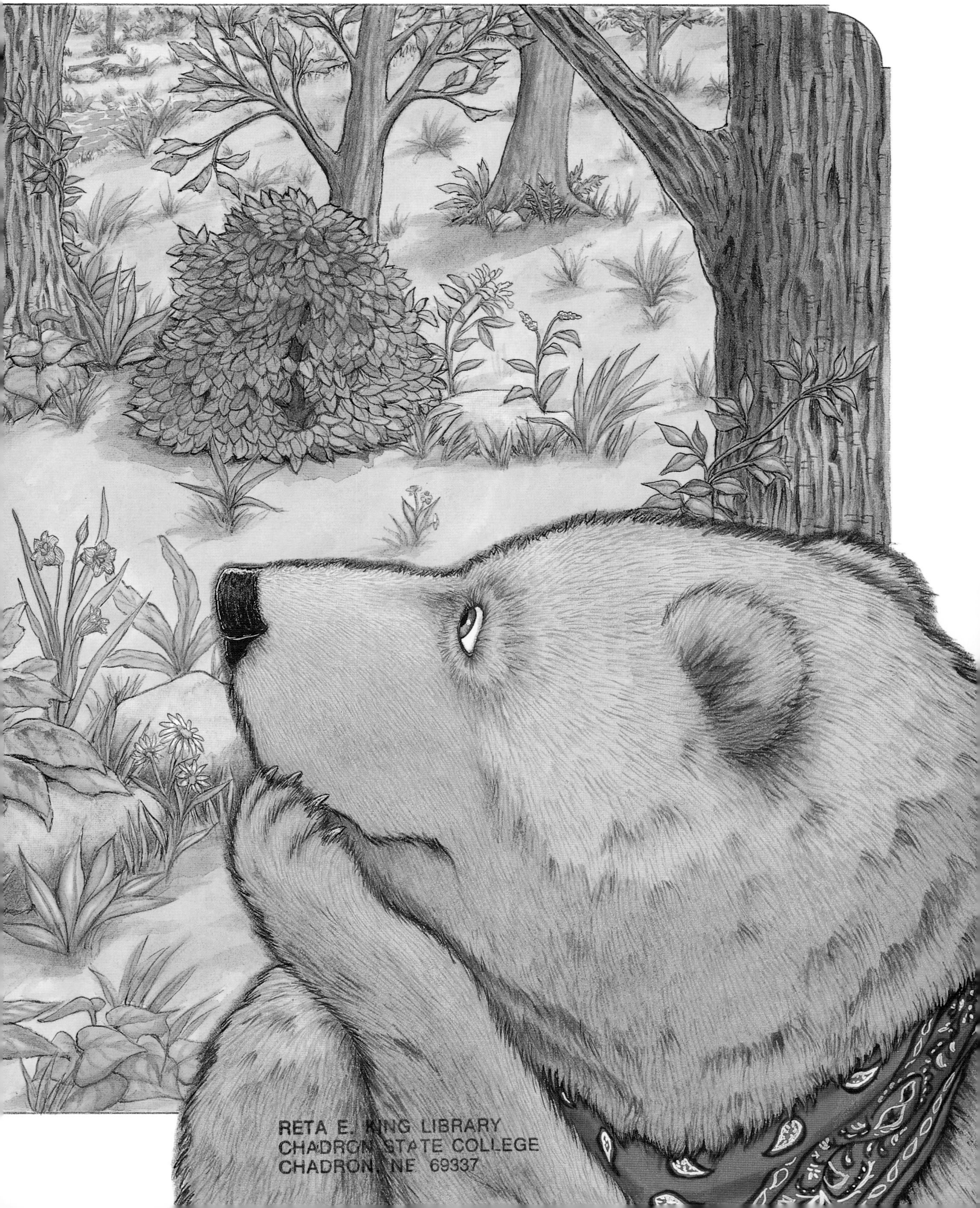

"Bear, you promised!"

Bear's friend Skunk had found him in the tall grass. She was frowning at him, scolding with her eyes. Bear gave her a sheepish look.

"The geese are sitting in a hole," Skunk told him. "They are sitting, making a strange sound. They say this is a golden age—a goose golden age."

Bear blinked at his friend.

"Bear, you have tricked the geese again. Promise you will go and rescue them." Bear promised he would rescue the geese from the goose hole the first thing in the morning.

The first thing in the morning there was a fog. Skunk walked in the fog to the riverbank, to a place near Bear's hole. She crept close. There was a gathering in the hole. Bear was there. The crickets and caterpillars were with him and so was Buffalo—with the trout in buckets. The geese were not there, but...but they were coming. Skunk saw them now. The geese were moving in the fog, walking gracefully, moving elegantly, with style and rhythm, in stockinged, slippered feet.

Skunk watched while the geese arranged themselves in the hole with Bear and Buffalo, with the trout and caterpillars and crickets. The gathering sat in silence in the fog, with bills and noses pointed skyward. But... but *was* it silence? Skunk seemed to hear a humming, a quiet humming. Skunk's eyes went out of focus. As she listened to the humming through the fog, her fur prickled. The humming was beautiful. It was harmonious. It made Skunk think of daffodils and snowflakes, of parachutes and waterfalls and choirs in a fog.

Skunk listened until the humming stopped, until the fog lifted, and the choir went home and Bear was by himself.

"Bear," she said, "it was good. The choir was good. You are good. But, Bear, were those geese and trout really singing?"

Bear gave his friend a sly look. He gave her a smile and a wink. "Yes and no," he answered.